HOME ALONe 2™

LOST IN NEW YORK

Kevin's Christmas Vacation Scrapbook

Adapted by Nancy E. Krulik
Based on the screenplay by John Hughes

SCHOLASTIC INC.
New York Toronto London Auckland Sydney

MW00885015

TWENTIETH CENTURY FOX PRESENTS A JOHN HUGHES PRODUCTION A CHRIS COLUMBUS FILM
MACAULAY CULKIN   JOE PESCI   DANIEL STERN   HOME ALONE 2
FILM EDITOR RAJA GOSNELL   PRODUCTION DESIGNER SANDY VENEZIANO   DIRECTOR OF PHOTOGRAPHY JULIO MACAT   EXECUTIVE PRODUCER MARK RADCLIFFE
HUGHES   DOLBY STEREO® IN SELECTED THEATRES   WRITTEN AND PRODUCED BY JOHN HUGHES   DIRECTED BY CHRIS COLUMBUS   COLOR BY DELUXE®
1991 TWENTIETH CENTURY FOX

These credits are tentative and subject to change.

ISBN 0-590-46187-7

Book designed by Ursula Herzog

12 11 10 9 8 7 6 5 4 3 2 1   2 3 4 5 6 7/9

Printed in the U.S.A.   24

First Scholastic printing, November 1992

My Christmas vacation started out really *lousy*! The very first night, my big brother Buzz made fun of me right in the middle of the school Christmas pageant!

So I let Buzz have it — right there, in front of everyone! Boy, were my folks mad! But I'd rather kiss a *toilet seat* than apologize to Buzz!

Last year my family spent most of their Christmas vacation in Paris with my uncle Rob. They remembered to bring along just about everything — except me!

This year I wasn't taking any chances. I didn't even stop to get batteries at the airport. I wanted to be sure I got on the plane to Florida with everyone else!

Wow

I got on the plane all right, just not on the *right* plane!
When my plane landed, my family was in Florida, but I was
in New York.
 Wow! All alone in the most exciting city in the world!

I knew right away which hotel to stay in. Maybe you've heard the TV commercials — "The Plaza Hotel, New York's most exciting hotel experience"?

Good thing I still had my dad's travel bag . . . and his wallet. I used his credit card to pay for my room! Pretty smart for a kid, huh?

Great room service!

The water's fine!

**All the comforts of home!
Now *this* is a vacation!**

Guests of the Plaza Hotel travel in style!
I really wish Buzz could have seen me in that limo!

Merry
X-Mas
Kevin

The driver took me to Duncan's Toy Chest. The place was awesome! And the owner was a real nice guy — every Christmas Eve he gives all the money he makes to the Children's Hospital to help sick kids have a good Christmas. I was glad to spend some of my money in his store!

Marv

Harry

Everything was going fine until I ran into these two jerks who tried to rob my house last Christmas. Back then they were no match for me! I hit them, tripped them, and smeared them with glue!

But now here they were in New York. This vacation was starting to seem an awful lot like last year's vacation!

I can't seem to get rid of these guys!

I thought I would be safe at the Plaza Hotel, New York's Most Exciting Hotel Experience. But the guy behind the desk thought I'd stolen my dad's wallet!

He threw me out — right into the arms of Harry and Marv!
AAAAAAAAAARGHGH! Then I threw *them* a little curve of my own!

Marv said I wasn't going to talk to anybody . . . except
maybe a fish! Yikes!
He also said they were gonna rob Duncan's Toy Chest!
(I don't think I was supposed to hear that part!)

They'll never learn.

Two bad guys were no match for the mighty Kevin
McCallister!

My uncle Rob has a house in New York. I ran there. I really hoped he was home from Paris already. But he wasn't! So there I was, at Uncle Rob's home — alone!

New York sure is a weird place. The pigeons outside Uncle
Rob's place were a lot nicer than the people I'd met!

The Pigeon Lady

Except for this one lady. She looked awful, but she really was okay. She just smelled like pigeons!

18

The Pigeon Lady was really lonely. She hardly ever talked to anybody. But she was a really good listener. I told her all about how I was always making my family mad at me.

The Pigeon Lady said that if you did a good deed, it made up for a lot of the rotten stuff you did. And on Christmas Eve, good deeds counted double!

I already knew what my good deed would be. But first I had to make sure Uncle Rob's house was ready for Harry and Marv. I made up a plan.

These wrenches might be good for something.

Ho Ho
Ho

I was sure they'd get
a bang out of these.

When I was through, I headed off to do my good deed. I was gonna make sure Harry and Marv didn't get any of the money Mr. Duncan was giving the sick kids at the hospital.

Say
Cheese!

Some folks just don't like to have their pictures taken!
Harry and Marv wanted that film before I gave it to the
police! They chased me all the way back to Uncle Rob's.

But as you already know, I was ready for them!
Hey guys — heads up!

Doesn't that color look great on him?

Harry and Marv got really mad after all that! I thought I was done for, until . . .

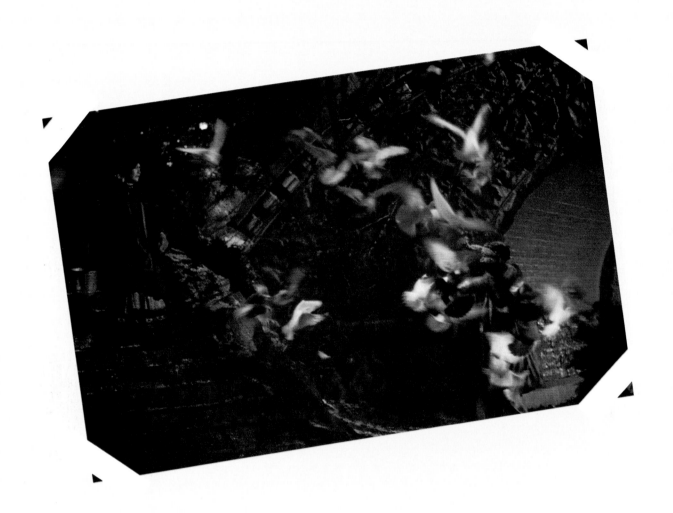

. . . the pigeon patrol came to the rescue!

Harry and Marv took a ride to the jailhouse with two of New York's Finest. And Mr. Duncan's money was safe. The sick kids would have a Christmas after all!

That was good news! But I was still all alone for Christmas. I knew I didn't deserve a Christmas, even though I had done a good deed. All I *really* wanted was to see my mother. . . .

Christmas wishes always come true!

Wow! This turned out to be the best Christmas vacation ever!